To my friend Liz – M.N.

A big piratey thank you to Mum and Dad – K.P.

First published 2004 by Macmillan Children's Books
This edition published 2005 by Macmillan Children's Books
a division of Macmillan Publishers Limited
20 New Wharf Road, London N1 9RR
Basingstoke and Oxford
Associated companies throughout the world
www.panmacmillan.com

ISBN: 978-1-4050-0916-4

5 7 9 8 6 4

A CIP catalogue record for this book
is available from the British Library.

Printed in China

Marjorie Newman

Captain Pike Looks After the Baby

Illustrated by Kate Pankhurst

MACMILLAN CHILDREN'S BOOKS

Mrs Pike was feeling frantic.
"I'll never finish this painting in time for Gran's birthday!" she cried. "The baby keeps me so busy!"
"Don't worry," said Captain Pike. "She can come with me on my pirate ship."

Mrs Pike looked at him. He was away at sea so much, he'd never tried taking care of the baby before.

"It will be easy-peasy!" said Captain Pike, packing the baby's things.

Proudly, Captain Pike carried the baby aboard the *Green Beetle*.
The crew looked at the baby.
"You can all help to take care of her," smiled Captain Pike.

Pirate snacks

The Gr

The crew looked at each other.
They said nothing.

The *Green Beetle* set sail. The baby cried.
"Grimstone!" said Captain Pike. "Change the baby!"
"Not me!" said Grimstone, holding his nose.
"I'm First Mate, not Baby Minder!"

The other pirates quickly
disappeared about their work.

Captain Pike changed
the baby himself.

He wasn't very
good at it.

The baby began
to cry again.

"Medlar!" shouted Captain Pike, taking the baby down to the galley. "The baby's hungry. Give her a bottle!"

"Not me!" cried Medlar. "I'm Ship's Cook, not Baby Minder! You don't want hungry pirates, do you?" Captain Pike shuddered at the thought.

Captain Pike fed
the baby himself.
She hiccuped a lot.
Then she cried.

Captain Pike rocked her...
He jiggled her...
He even tried singing to her.

At last he put her on his
shoulder and patted her back.
The baby gave an enormous

Burp!

Then she snuggled down in Captain Pike's arms and went to sleep.
"Hush everyone!" ordered Captain Pike softly.
"Don't wake the baby!"

"Pirate ship approaching!" the lookout whispered, loudly.
It was the *Blue Raider*. On board were their deadly enemies,
Captain Whitebeard and his crew.
"Get ready to fight!" said Grimstone.

Captain Whitebeard and his crew jumped aboard the *Green Beetle*, yelling and shouting.

Captain Pike's crew yelled and shouted even more.

Captain Pike rushed to his cabin door.

"STOP THAT NOISE!"

he bellowed.

"YOU'LL WAKE THE BABY!"

The pirates froze.
And then . . .

"Now you've woken her up yourself!" chuckled Captain Whitebeard.

After that, there was no more fighting.
Captain Whitebeard, who loved children
and had ten of his own, stayed all day.

He bathed and changed
and fed the baby.

He played peep-bo
with her . . .

and sang her a lullaby.

Captain Pike learned a lot.

And the other pirates soon discovered that it was much more fun to be friends than to fight all the time.

They compared cutlasses, swapped treasure maps, and sang sea shanties, while Medlar brought round lots of delicious food and drink.

At last, the *Blue Raider* sailed away,
and Captain Pike set course for a short trip
round the islands.

map of islands →

baby bib

He had a busy time,
doing two jobs at once.

At the end of the voyage,
Captain Pike carried
the baby ashore.
"How was it?" asked Mrs Pike.

"Easy-peasy!" said Captain Pike.

But then he yawned, wearily.
Mrs Pike looked at him . . .

Then she began to laugh.

Captain Pike looked at her.
He began to laugh, too.

"Well, maybe it wasn't easy-peasy,"
he spluttered at last.
"But I'd do it again, any time!"

And he gave them both
a great big piratey hug!